Sunflower Field

AUTHOR: BRIDGET HOLDER
ILLUSTRATOR: ALEXANDRIA SEARLE

Print information available on the last page.

Rev. date: 07/09/2019

To order additional copies of this book, contact:
Xlibris
1-888-795-4274
www.Xlibris.com
Orders@Xlibris.com

This book is dedicated to my children
Kenny and Lauryn

Never give up.

Abby has a plan. She loves sunflowers.
She wants to grow her own field
of tall, yellow sunflowers.

Abby's parents have an empty field.
They told Abby if she wants to grow
sunflowers she will have to do all the
work to prepare them in the field.

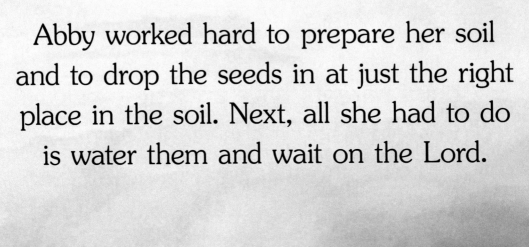

Abby worked hard to prepare her soil
and to drop the seeds in at just the right
place in the soil. Next, all she had to do
is water them and wait on the Lord.

He's working
on her behalf.

She believed, even when
she couldn't see.

Then just at the right time....

While she had been waiting patiently....

She began to see God's grace.

She began to worship him.

He's not done yet.

Because of her faithfulness....

...others will know that she's blessed.

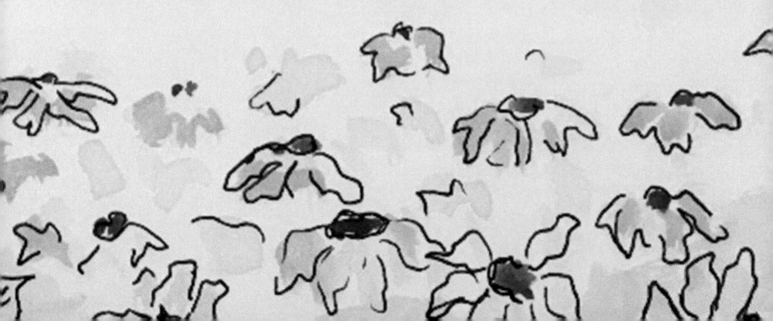

Printed in the United States
By Bookmasters